Sniff-whiff. Clara Kitten is a super-sniffer. She loves to smell things.

But sometimes, her nose gets her into trouble — like the time it led her to the wonderful-smelling oranges in the grocery store. Sniff-whiff went Clara's nose. Rumble-tumble went the oranges.

You can smell the oranges, too, if you scratch and sniff them. Then turn the page, and see if Clara's nose leads her into more trouble.

ORANGES

APPLES

A Nose for Trouble

by Barbara Shook Hazen
pictures by Tim and Greg Hildebrandt

gb Golden Press • New York

Western Publishing Company, Inc.
Racine, Wisconsin

Clara Kitten seemed to have a nose for trouble.
Things were always happening to her.

One day she made blueberry pie all by herself.
When it was baked, Clara called, "Mother! Father!
Come see what I made. Doesn't it smell delicious?"
And she leaned over to sniff the pie.

Scratch and sniff.
How do you like the smell
of Clara's blueberry pie?

Suddenly Clara slipped. Her elbow bumped the pie plate.

Crash! Splat! Clara's beautiful pie fell to the floor.

Clara looked at the messy blue puddle. "Oh no," she wailed, "I've done it again."

"Never mind," said her mother. "You run outside and play. I'll clean up. But please — try to keep your nose out of trouble."

THE CATS'MEOW

Scratch and sniff.
Don't the lilacs smell like springtime!

Clara climbed a wall, kicked a stone
and blew the fuzz off some dandelion tops.
Then, sniff-whiff, her nose led her
to a lilac bush.
"Oh, I love the smell of lilacs,"
said Clara. She buried her
nose in the blossoms.

"Ouch!" yelled Clara. "Who bit me?"
"I did," buzzed an angry bee. "It's my
lilac bush. I got here first. Besides, making
honey is my business. You just keep your
nose out of my business, Clara Cat."

Clara ran down to the brook. She splashed
her sore nose with cold water.

And then, sniff-whiff, Clara's nose caught
the scent of something else nice — pizza,
a wonderful cheesy pizza left on a log.

"I wonder who left it there?" said Clara.
She leaned over to take a closer sniff.

Scratch and sniff the pizza
Clara found.
Doesn't that smell make
you hungry?

All at once the log leapt to life.

"Ho, ho, hee, hee," howled Alvin Alligator. "Stop tickling me with your whiskers."

As he laughed, the pizza slid off his back and splashed into the brook. "Now look what you've done," snapped Alvin. "My beautiful pizza is ruined. Please Clara, take your nose somewhere else."

Scratch and sniff the mint leaves.
Have you ever tried mint in
lemonade?

"What a rotten day," sighed Clara. "Nothing's gone right. I think I'll go over to Benjamin's house. At least he's still my friend."

Clara took a short cut by an empty house. Sniff-whiff, Clara's nose led her to a mint bed by the back porch.

"Mint smells wonderful," said Clara, "and it tastes good, too. I'll pick some for Benjamin. We'll put it in our lemonade."

Clara had picked two fistfuls when someone screeched,
"Whooo's there? Whooo's picking my mint?"

The someone was an old owl, full of fuss and feathers,
who lived all alone in the attic.

She looked like a ghost as she came flapping out of
the window. Clara was so startled she dropped the
mint and ran the rest of the way to Benjamin's house.

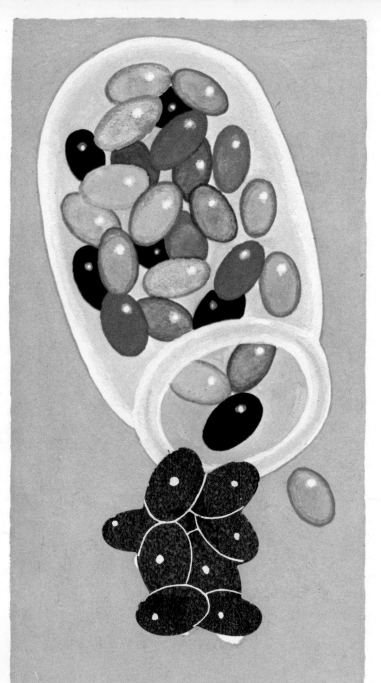

Scratch and sniff the licorice jelly beans.
Is licorice your favorite flavor, too?

"It's been an awful day," Clara told Benjamin. "All day long my nose has gotten me into trouble."

"That's too bad," said Benjamin. "Have a jelly bean. Jelly beans make anything better. I got a whole jar for my birthday."

"I like licorice best," said Clara. Sniff-whiff. She stuck her face into the jar.

Alas, the jar stuck on Clara's nose. To get it unstuck, Clara had to soak her nose in soapy water.

"Fine friend you are," said Benjamin. "Now they're ruined." He looked at the sink full of soapy jellybeans.

"But I didn't mean to get my nose that far in," said Clara. "I'll make it up to you."

"I'll bet," said Benjamin.

Clara felt miserable. She went straight home. No one was there.

Clara lay on her bed. "If I never leave my room," she said, "my nose can't get me into any more trouble."

Suddenly she smelled something sharp and strong. It was coming from the kitchen.

Clara ran to the telephone. She dialed 0 — just as her mother had told her to do in case of trouble.

"This is Clara Cat," she said. "I live at 108 Catnip Lane. I'm all alone and I smell smoke. Please hurry!"

Scratch and sniff.
Can you smell the smoke, too?

When Mr. and Mrs. Cat got back from their shopping, they saw the fire engines in front of the house.

That was when Mrs. Cat remembered she had left the oven on.

"Lucky you have such an alert youngster," said Fire Chief Dan Dalmatian. "If Clara hadn't smelled the smoke, we wouldn't have caught the fire in time."